ROSIE KNOWS *more*

MORE ADVENTURES OF AN ORDINARY DOG

ROSIE RUBIN

Balboa Press books may be ordered through booksellers or by contacting:

Balboa Press
A Division of Hay House
1663 Liberty Drive
Bloomington, IN 47403
www.balboapress.com.au
1 (877) 407-4847

ISBN: 978-1-5043-1624-8 (sc)
ISBN: 978-1-5043-1625-5 (e)

Print information available on the last page.

Balboa Press rev. date: 12/21/2018

BALBOA
PRESS
A DIVISION OF HAY HOUSE

CONTENTS

CLOUDS COME AND GO

Rosie here again

How are you going my human readers?

I know you are there because I get emails from you which Miss Polly reads and she gets as excited as I do!

It has been such an amazing time for me with so many changes!

I will tell you more in the pages of this new book

I am never quite sure if I like changes as some can be good and others pretty scary.

Nevada says that change natural and there will always be changes.

He remembers when he was a little pup and the world seemed so scary but now he is a big dog and he is more confident.

Oh! Nevada you are such a smart dog! I love you to bits!

Nevada says every day has something different on the menu and even yesterday is never exactly the same as today.

As for tomorrow, well Nevada says that is too far away to worry about!

Nevada says humans worry more than dogs but I am not sure if I understand that word.

I do notice that humans change their facial expression more than we dogs ..but of course humans don't have tails to wag which could be the problem.

Sometimes humans wear their smile upside down which seems to be a signal for us dogs to stay close to the ground and not jump up to play.

Nevada says that humans get stressed and it changes their outlook on life for a while.

I do understand that word stress as I get stressed with those pesky crows but I think Nevada meant the kind of stress that seems to affect how humans allow themselves to enjoy life.

Perhaps that is worry?

I remember when Miss Polly was stressed.

She lost her purse and phone and was walking from one room to another opening cupboards and drawers and she even went to the hen house to see if she had left it there.

She was not her usual happy self and she did not stop to pat me even when I gave her my cutest look.

Her worrying seemed to last forever and made me feel quite sad like when it is a cloudy day or raining and cold. I tried to wag my tail but it was difficult.

All ended up ok though as her telephone rang and she was able to hear it.

Do you know where it was?

It was in the car underneath my doggy blanket!!!

I could have told her that if she would have asked!

Of course there are some changes that are really big like when your best friend leaves on a plane to live far away... or when someone you love dies!

That can make you feel sad, like the sun is stuck behind the clouds all day.

Pedro my doggy friend had an eye injury some time ago and it was pretty upsetting at the time but now he can do most things like before, except he has to turn his head more!

So it seems that Nevada is right again and this is all part of the way life is.

He is right too when he says it is how you look at it.

Like Pedro looking through one good eye!! He! He!

Nevada says the sun is always shining but sometimes we just can't remember it is there because of our our problems...which are like clouds.

But have you noticed that clouds are always changing and then the sun comes out again.

So my lovely friends, if your worry clouds are hiding your sun just remember that it will change.

Right now the sun is shining warmly on my glossy coat and Nevada is digging a hole so I will go and help!!

Bye for now!

Rosie

AS TIME GOES BY

Hello its Rosie again!!

How are you today? I have something to tell you that makes my tail wag so much.

I have been on a special outing with Miss Polly to see a group of older people who live all together in a big house with a garden and lots of rooms...not a hospital, but it did smell a bit too clean. (At least for dogs!)

It was a place where older humans go to be together and have other humans help them with their daily chores, cook their meals and that sort of thing

Some of these humans were pretty old and although some did walk on their own paws most of them sat in chairs with wheels. I saw a few of these humans walking really slowly as they pushed some strange looking metal frames on little wheels, and I had to be quick to make sure my paws did not get run over!!

Everyone was really happy to see me and gave me lots of pats and scratches on my neck.

One lady even wanted to knit me a colourful woollen doggy coat!! She said she used to have a dog called Rosie!

There was a piano in the corner of this big room and someone playing really nice music, not like I hear normally on the radio, but slow music with soft singing.

I could see that these older people were not able to get out into their paddocks and run like I can and I also noticed that some could not see or hear too well either.

I do not know many older dogs in this town but I do know that the more birthdays we dogs have the slower we get.

The same for humans eh?

Some of the humans looked a little sad and lonely and said that their family were very busy and did not get to visit them very often. One man told Miss Polly that he had no family at all, which surprised me.

Most of these older humans smiled at me when I did cool things like sit, stay, lay down, come when I was called. I was a super well behaved dog of course, using my best manners.

I admit I did show off a bit!

I even refused a biscuit that one man kindly offered, that was difficult because it was a creamy one and I really wanted it - but I know Miss Polly has rules about taking food from people.

I could see Miss Polly was proud of me.

When we left I waved my paw to say goodbye all the people did not want me to go, so Miss Polly promised that she would bring me back again another time and they all cheered!!

That felt good!

Even the caring ladies in the big house all wanted to pat me but I could see that they were busy with their work as they were laying the tables for dinner.

On the way home I started to think of how lucky I am and I felt so grateful to have friends and family who care about me.

I began to appreciate being young and fit enough to enjoy life too, something I had not really thought about before.

That's when my tail started to wag... and wag... and wag! I was feeling grateful for all that I have

Miss Polly calls it an "Attitude of Gratitude" which is much the same as tail wagging in my doggy world!

Please remember to be happy and have fun...one day you may be older and have time to sit and remember all these good times.

I think I will go and find that meaty bone I buried last week!!

Yum!

Talk soon

Rosie

BATH TIME ...AGAIN!!

Hello again from Rosie.

Grrr!

Its bath time again!!

I just don't get it...it makes no sense to us dogs.

Is it any surprise to you that when I see the black plastic tub and the smelly dog shampoo bottle I try to hide? Wouldn't you?

All those wonderful smells on my glossy coat washed away by shampoo that makes me smell like a bunch of flowers! I am a DOG! - Dogs like to smell like dogs, why don't you humans get it?

Standing in the tub is so embarrassing. Miss Polly doesn't trust me to do it willingly so she has to lift me into the tub and keep the leash around my collar because I would jump out, wouldn't you?

I get wet all over, covered in soapy stuff that seems to want to make me go blind, and then it is all washed off again! Please tell me where is the sense in that??

It has always puzzled me that humans rush to put on coats and umbrellas when it is raining outside to and yet go into the house to deliberately get wet!??

Miss Polly stands in the shower or takes a bath when we have plenty of water and she even likes it. Humans are so difficult to understand.

Some time ago,when I was a pup, I jumped into a horse trough.

My eyes and ears filled up with water, sooo scary!

I got out ok. I shook my ears and my wet glossy coat, then rolled a few times in the grass and felt much better. I decided never to get into water tubs again, but here I am having a bath!

But wait... the craziness of this ritual does not stop there!

Don't you think that it makes sense to shake and roll when your glossy coat is soaking wet?

Miss Polly says I have to be rubbed down with a towel (I can handle that ok) and then I must stand still until I am dry!

Even a dog knows that a wet glossy coat will smell better with nice smelly cow manure to roll in.

How is it that humans don't seem to understand simple stuff like that?

The only good thing about the whole procedure is that I get my coat brushed and it does feel good, except my tail... that is a sensitive part. I will tell you about that another time

Miss Polly says that she wants me to look good and smell good because it shows respect to others by making an effort not to look scruffy!

She should meet my old friend who lives in Queensland!

Now he IS scruffy, he is actually called Scruffy by his owners.

Scruffy was an orphan before he was found by a family to love him, just like me!

He had no care at all and I must say even we dogs noticed how sad and untidy he looked.

He was lost for a long time and survived on scraps of food he could find in the garbage bins.

Sometimes he did not eat for days and he looked like a wild dog always angry and had no friends.

He has a good home now but he still looks scruffy and when his new owners try to bath him he growls and runs away for days.

I have to say I am lucky not to walk on his paws

I am washed and brushed regularly which shows me that Miss Polly cares.

I forgot to mention that I usually get a special treat to chew after all this bath suffering!

I am learning that some things have to be accepted because the benefits are more than the downsides.

I guess you have similar situations in your world, like doing homework, eating your veggies and getting clean and dressed in nice clothes to go to church or when Nana comes to visit.

Miss Polly is right (again!) It is a way of showing respect, that you think enough of others (and yourself) to make an effort.

I can handle the compliments like "Oh! You look so pretty today Rosie" and all the pats on my nice clean, and glossy coat!

I guess it is worth the suffering after all!

Oops! I had better go now as I can see Miss Polly has the nail clippers in her hand!!

Yelps!

Woofs!

🐾 FRIENDS AND SHARING 🐾

Hello again my human friends

Rosie here!

I hope you are enjoying my adventures.

I always have so much to tell you and it is so good to get your emails too. Thank you!

The email Harley sent to me with the drawing of a big meaty bone wrapped up in a big pink bow looked so delicious that I wanted to chew it,but Miss Polly said it was not real and print out paper was not good for a dog to eat!

Thank you also to the teacher who wrote to say that I was the best behaved dog in class when I visited the school last week. The children in her class were all very respectful and quiet when Miss Polly read my story. I usually sit while Miss Polly talks but the students look at me mostly because I am so cute!! I love going to schools!

Afterward school Miss Polly took me to visit Buster who lives in town and she sat talking to Busters owner while having a cool drink on the porch.

Buster and I raced around the yard playing chasey and hide and seek.

Charlie came calling too with another little fluffy puppy, but I can't quite remember her name.

It was such fun and we were careful not to play too rough with the fluffy puppy.

Suddenly we heard some angry barks from two big dogs next door.

They did not like us having fun and they started jumping up at the fence and growling.

Buster knew them well and warned me to stay away as the last time they got out of their yard they chased a car and almost knocked down an elderly lady.

That is not good dog behaviour.

Buster said that if they came into his yard they would try to fight and be mean.

I have already learned not to go near mean dogs and I have a few scars on my super sensitive nose to prove it.

He said "They just don't play nice." I have realised that fighting is best avoided altogether, so I walk away, even run!

Charlie the big black Labrador has lots of energy but I know he would never hurt me. He rolls me onto my back sometimes when we play but he always licks me to say "RU Ok Rosie".

It shows me he cares.

Fluffy dog is so small she could fit into Busters mouth, but he is always careful not to scare her. Buster always plays fair, in fact we dogs call him the gentle giant!

I enjoy playing with Buster and Charlie and fluffy dog and I know they are happy to be my friend too. I have learned to choose my friends carefully and to value them because good friends are worth keeping.

I wish those dogs behind the fence would learn that they need to be kind and play fair if they want true friendship. Being mean is no fun and if sometimes dogs are mean to us we just walk away and ignore them. Who wants to be friends with a mean dog??

I am thinking that is the same in humans' world, right?

Of course you know all this but I just wanted you to know how much I am learning.

Talk soon

Rosie

DREAMS AND ADVENTURES

Hi again! Rosie here!

Have you ever noticed that we dogs sleep a lot?

We like to lie down often to rest our body and our brain.

On a warm sunny day there is nothing nicer than to find a nice shady tree, tuck my nose into my paws and have a doggy nap. It is like recharging our battery and storing up energy to do things like chase crows or run after rabbits!

Sometimes I sleep deeply but mostly I have one ear open to sounds around me or if Miss Polly calls.

I enter into my doggy thoughts and imagine all sorts of adventures, a bit like your dreams perhaps?

I dream of chasing cars with big wheels (something I am never allowed to do in real life!) and sometimes I dream of being a flying dog, able to catch those crows up in the high branches of the trees.

Of course it seems real but I know it is not once I wake up.

Not long ago I had a really scary adventure and it seemed so real that I got quite frightened.

Let me tell you about it.

In my dream, I was being chased by a pack of hungry wolves in a strange place

My legs were sore from running away, as they were closing in on me and were super fast, almost flying!

I ran through a jungle of trees and fell over branches, hurting my paws, but I had to keep going as I knew that if they caught up with me I would be a dead dog!!

I ran as fast as I could and when I got through the forest I found that I was in a big open space which seemed to go forever.

I was so tired and my heart was beating fast, my tongue was dry from panting, when suddenly the path I was following came to an end and before me there was ....nothing!!

I was standing on the edge of a great big cliff .

Nowhere to go but down!

I could not see the bottom as it was foggy with clouds.

I could hear the pack of wolves getting closer and louder with their dog howls, which in doggy language means "We have got you now ....and you are DEAD!"

I was so terrified and really thought that this was the end of my doggy life!

What could I do?

I had to make a decision. Would I stay and get mauled to death or would I jump to my probable death into the ravine? Not an easy decision eh?

I closed my eyes very tightly, took a deep breath and jumped off the cliff falling fast through the clouds and hoping it would not hurt too much when I hit the ground.

Bump...!!!!!

I woke up under the shady tree wondering where I was.

But soon realised that I had been dreaming!

I was so wobbly on my legs I could not walk too well and my tail did not remember how to wag..in fact I was shaking all over.

That dream seemed so real...but I was glad to be alive!

It took me a while to get my tail wagging again so I went over to Miss Polly for a pat just to feel connected to the real world again.

I am not sure why I had that dream, perhaps it was a movie I was watching last week with Miss Polly, or was it was listening to some of the older farm dogs telling scary stories ?.

I don't know really but I do know that once I woke up I was safe.

Perhaps next time I am in a dream like that I will try to remember that it is just a dream and tell myself to wake up.

Oh! I have to go now as it is time to put the hens away and then Miss Polly will put my dinner into the big silver doggy dish,....I think it is lamb stew and veggies tonight..My favourite!

Happy Dreams

Rosie

THUNDER AND LIGHTENING... VERY VERY FRIGHTENING!

Hellooooo...It's Rosie here and I am talking *very quietly.*

Ssshh! I don't want anyone to see me!

I am pretty scared right now and I am sure I can share this with you as you have been scared too.

It all started this afternoon when my super sensitive ears heard a rumbling noise all around and it was getting closer. I think you call it thunder.

I have known this before once when I was a pup and it was scary then too.

I was with my mother then and we pups snuggled up really close to her even though she was shaking too!

I am feeling so alone and I miss my Mum and brothers right now

I am hiding under Miss Polly's bed and although I know she wants me to come out,I feel safer here in the dark. I just feel too scared and to tell the truth I feel a little embarrassed.

I will just stay here until I stop shaking and hope that the bed does not fall in on me and I will be a trapped dog! Strange isn't it that when you are scared of one thing, other things become scary too!

Here I am thinking the bed will collapse...how dumb is that? But fear does that.

I even jumped up when I saw my black shiny tail and thought it was a snake!

I hit my head on the bed base!

It would be funny if it were not so scary!!

It is good to talk with you as I feel that I am not so alone and that you understand.

What do you do when you feel scared like this?

I know Miss Polly would want me to come out from under the bed and let her pat me and say nice calm words, but right now it is enough just to know she cares.

It is not that I don't trust her, but I am too scared even to do anything!

My mind is so mixed up and I keep thinking the next lightening flash will bring a louder boom of thunder to hurt my super sensitive ears. The world could end!

In fact the last boom was not quite so loud but the next one might be, so I will prepare my mind and expect the worst!

BOOM! I am still shaking.

I remember my Mum said to me that if I let my whole body go floppy and pretend I am in a warm, safe place it will help but I tried that already and I am still shaking.

I feel exhausted as if I have been chasing rabbits all day....instead I have been sitting here shaking and scared under the bed.

This thunder seems so big; I will never be able to stop it.

What can I do I am just a dog!?

Perhaps it is not about me stopping it, that's impossible, but what if I stopped fighting it!

I will try just *allowing* it and not resisting... which does not mean I have to like it!

Oh! Oh!

Here it comes again, a big flash coming through the window and lighting up the room. Even from under the bed I can see it!

I will wait for the thunder noise but try not to resist it. Just relax my brain and know that I can do it! Breathing will help I think.

Long slow breaths ....one... two...

Booooom!

My ears are still hurting from that one which I think was louder than the last, but guess what!

I am feeling ok, even though I still wish it were all over.

Somehow my mind is not so blurry but I think I can manage one more, and that is as far as I am going to think.

Oh! Dear!

Sorry for that pause in talking I think I must have fallen asleep, and all is quiet.

It is getting darker now and I have been under this bed for a while.

Miss Polly is encouraging me to come out and she has some nice doggy treats. I know she means well and wants to help me.

I have learned something today, that no one else can overcome my fears but me!

Even though Miss Polly loves me and wants to help, it is really up to me isn't it?

I am not saying I won't be scared again when I hear that thunder, but I think I have a plan for next time. I wonder if it will work on Firecracker night!

That could be a whole new challenge!

Right now I feel happier and just a bit proud of myself!

Thanks for being there my human friends.

You have helped me help myself!

Love

Rosie

Ps: The slow breaths did help a lot!

WHAT'S THE DIFFERENCE?

Rosie here again

Have you got time to hear about my day?

I do hope you like hearing about my doggy world?

I was telling my friends Buster, Charlie and Fluffy dog about you all and they send woofs and tail wags to you !

What I like about my friends is that they like me even though I am different to them.

We dogs are all sorts of breeds and although we all have four legs and waggy tails and shiny black wet noses we are quite different.

Charlie is very black and shiny and has the whitest teeth, Buster is white with brown patches and half his face is brown and half is white with big black spots on his ears and Fluffy dog just looks like one of those feather dusters that humans use to polish their precious ornaments!

I am different too, just look at my photo on the back cover. I have one blue eye and one brown eye!

That is quite unusual but my great Uncle Ben had different colour eyes too so it is a family thing.

I think that I am a fine looking dog with a glossy black coat and I am more of a sporty dog than my friends. Some tell me that I should be a racetrack dog because I can run fast and change direction on a penny! I don't think I even ran across a penny!

My breed of dog has been working for many years mustering sheep on the farms here in Australia. We have developed a talent for knowing how to get big flocks of sheep into fenced yards for shearing.

My Great Uncle Ben was a famous sheep dog performing at the Royal Easter Show in Sydney. He was well known in all of New South Wales and I am proud to be named after my Great Aunt Rosie who was with him for many years and had many pups together.

I know this is the same in your human world too because I see so many students at school and in town with different skin colours and hair colours and all sizes and shapes.

We dogs accept it as normal and in fact although we are each proud of our own heritage, we respect every other dogs right to be proud of theirs.

Gigi is a French Poodle and she has beautiful curls. She has been a show dog in the city and quite often she wears a cute pink bow in her hair and walks like a model on her tiny black shiny toes.

We all love Gigi because she is always giggling and telling stories of the big city. She even speaks differently and says things like "Vive la Difference" which she says is the same as I have been trying to say!

Gigi is always good at explaining stuff, even though at times we cannot understand her accent!!

Dogs and humans are so lucky to live in a world of endless variety and we all make up a wonderful community.

It would be so boring if we were all the same don't you think?

Doggy love and licks

Rosie

LIFE'S LEARNING

Hello again

Rosie here!

I am sooo ready for my holidays, are you?

I know some of you are leaving town to visit friends and family and one student told me that he is going in a plane over to another country!

Yelps!

I think I would prefer to stay on the ground!

I watch those big planes that look like big birds with silver wings.

I know that humans travel across the sky regularly but I guess that is something humans can do better than dogs.

Where do you keep your wings I wonder?

Miss Polly says that this year seems to have been longer than usual, and she could be right but dogs don't really know much about time. Except dinnertime of course!

School seems to have been very busy lately, a lot of serious faces which is unusual.

Miss Polly says it is "Exam time" whatever that is?

I saw a sign outside one of the classrooms saying "Quiet please, exams in progress" so I thought that some of the students in there must have had a headache?

One student looked very upset coming out of this room. She was crying and she let me lick up the salty tears that kept falling onto her knees. We sat for a while together and she told me that she was feeling sore in the head and tummy and I could feel she was shaking.

She told me that she seemed to forget everything she was supposed to know.

The exam headache must have passed now because I saw some of the students in town today, laughing and feeling very happy. They were celebrating a "graduation" like it was a birthday.

"Exams over" must be a special time in the human year like Christmas or Thanksgiving??

We dogs don't have exams of course.

All that is required for us to know is that we are deserving of whatever life has to offer, and happiness is natural. We do not need an exam to prove that!

Our happiness is not about competing or feeling that we have to be as good as anyone else. We are ok with making mistakes because that is the only way we dogs learn.

In a dog's world, what you humans call success and failure is all part of growing up, a natural pathway to becoming the best dog we can be. Some dogs learn faster than others.

Charlie is a great example, he is such a smart dog without even trying. We all know he is smart and remind him that he only has one tail to wag, just like the rest of us.

Buster does not feel a failure because he can't swim or catch a ball in his mouth like Charlie.

I am proud that I am the fastest dog in our group but never let Fluffy feel bad because she is the slowest. Life is not meant to be a competition in our doggy world.

We do our best and then keep improving! Simple eh?

Ah! Yes, I was talking about holidays before that confusing exam word.

Miss Polly is going to take a break from her work in school for a while and that means we will have more time to go for walks and fun stuff, but I know I will miss seeing all the students.

It seems to me that some humans are busier on their holidays than when they are at work or school, so I hope to hear all the stories of your adventures when next we meet.

Adventures are just another way of learning wouldn't you say?

Even more fun sometimes too!!

Most important for us dogs is knowing that each day holds new opportunities to live life!

It's all about having a go! (As we Aussie dogs say!)

I think it would be similar for humans.

Let me know!

Wagging my tail to you..

Woofs

Rosie

GRRR!   🐾

Hello again...Rosie here.

Have you got a minute?

I need help!!

It's about this new harness that Miss Polly has bought for me to wear...Ugh!!

I do NOT like it!

It's itchy on my nose and I think it is designed to stop me from pulling Miss Polly along when I am on the leash. The problem is that she walks too slowly for me!

I want to get as much ground under my paws as possible.... more ground... more smells to sniff ...obvious isn't it? This new harness slows me up.

Grrr! I would like to chew it to bits, or bury it where no one will ever find it.

My friend Charlie the big black Labrador has a harness and I suspect that is where Miss Polly got the idea. Charlie walks slowly on the leash and his owner Miss Nikki does not have to pull on his neck collar.

I must say he looks good.

People meet him and say "what a good dog". He just wags his tail and feels good about himself!

Miss Nikki gives him lots of pats for being a smart dog and his collar is not so tight anymore!

Charlie says he feels better because he knows that Miss Nikki is happy with him and he is quite content to walk slowly on the leash because once the harness is off he can run free, as fast as likes!

Will I ever feel that way?

Miss Polly is concerned that I might run into the road and chase those big truck wheels, or that somebody in the street might trip over me and fall... but a harness is going a bit too far isn't it?

Of course Gigi just loves her harness and walks along the street with her head held high,wagging her Pom Pom tail, and feeling very special, but I am a sheep dog and we are born to run free!

Miss Polly explained that sometimes we all have to do things we do not like but we must look at the bigger picture and how this training can help in the future.

I am guessing that it is the same for students at school.

Are there times when you don't want to finish a school project or assignment and would prefer to go play ball with your friends? Who wants to clean up your bedroom when your favourite TV show is on!

Yes I think I get it.

Miss Polly wants me to be the best dog I can be and to be honest I want that too.

I just wish it did not include slow walking.

But if Charlie can do it then so can I because now Charlie walks on the leash without it the harness!!

Thanks for listening.

Rosie

THE BIG THREE

Hello again

This is Rosie woofing to tell you about a very special woof-day!

I have a birthday in a few days time.

It happens every year, but this is super special because I am going to be three!

The Big Three! In our doggy world it means I am grown up, a mature dog, a bit like when humans get to reach twenty one.

Actually I do not feel any different but Miss Polly tells me that I should wear a special badge because next week at school there will be a lot more pats than usual.

Who would not want that?

Being three is quite a responsibility and because I will be a mature dog I get to do cool things like chew bigger meaty bones, stay up later in the evening (the best time to chase rabbits) and wear a new big dog collar with a silver buckle.

I also get to tell younger pups what to do because I will be wiser.

When my friend Missy comes to visit she will have to listen to me. She is a city dog and I think she is a bit spoilt (quietly) and she always wants her own way.

She scratches the door to come in and jumps up on Miss Polly's legs for attention.

She even begs for food when her owner Harry is sitting at the dinner table!

I will have to have some stern words to her now that I am a mature dog.

She will have to watch me and learn better manners.

I will show her fun things too like how to bury a bone so that other dogs won't find it and she will have to show me respect or I will growl at her to say I am not pleased.

Of course I would never hurt Missy, she is a small dog and we dogs have a rule that we must never hurt younger or smaller dogs.

Is that the same in your human world?

There is also other stuff that I am expected to do which is not so cool like be more obedient, not bark at cars and stop my jumping up and licking behaviour.

I am not sure how I will be able to do that but Miss Polly will want me to try.

Having more birthdays means growing up, even though in many ways it would be cool to be a cute puppy forever.

Miss Polly says that growing up comes with responsibilities and I have to become an example to younger pups and teach them the right way to do things so that means that *I have to do things right!*

Yelps!

I am not sure this growing up is so cool after all!

I imagine that this is similar for humans, especially when graduating from school years.

There will always be things that you are expected to know and be an example to other students.

New students need to learn where to put their school bag and to remember to put their hand up in class to talk and not shout out. I think it is good to show younger pups the right way to behave just like older friends showed you. I guess it also works with younger siblings!

Just make sure to be kind because learning new stuff is not easy.

Don't I know it!!!

I am happy to be growing up although I know I will still have to listen to older dogs and I will be learning for a while yet. It's quite exciting!

But right now I am still a pup for a few more days and I can still be silly!!

I am off to roll in the grass and get very smelly,dig holes under the fence and chase those pesky crows!! He! He!

This is the end of my book.

Thank you for listening to my stories and please come again because in my next book "What Rosie Knows" I will be sharing the adventures of a mature dog!

Woofs, licks and wags

Your friend

Rosie!

Printed in the United States
By Bookmasters